The Case of the

Stolen Sixpence

For Jon, Cam, Robin, and Will
—H.W.

For Janine and Kath, with much love
—M.L.

Text copyright © 2014 by Holly Webb
Illustrations copyright © 2014 by Marion Lindsay

Originally published by Stripes Publishing, an imprint of Little Tiger Press,
Great Britain, in 2013. All rights reserved.

For information about permission to reproduce selections from this book,
write to Permissions, Houghton Mifflin Harcourt Publishing Company,
215 Park Avenue South, New York, New York 10003.

www.hmhco.com

Library of Congress Cataloging-in-Publication Data
Webb, Holly.
The case of the stolen sixpence / written by Holly Webb;
illustrated by Marion Lindsay.
p. cm. — (The mysteries of Maisie Hitchins)
Originally published by Stripes Publishing, an imprint of Little Tiger Press,
Great Britain, in 2013.
Summary: Junior sleuth Maisie Hitchins, who lives in her grandmother's boarding
house in Victorian London, uncovers an intriguing plot involving stolen sausages,
pilfered halfpennies, and a fast-paced bicycle chase.
ISBN 978-0-544-33928-6 hardback
[1. Mystery and detective stories. 2. Boardinghouses—Fiction. 3. London (England)—
History—19th century—Fiction. 4. Great Britain—History—Victorian, 1837–1901—
Fiction.] I. Lindsay, Marion, illustrator. II. Title.
PZ7.W3687Cap 2014
[Fic]—dc23
2014007446

Printed in the United States of America
DOC 10 9 8 7 6 5 4 3 2 1
4500485092

THE MYSTERIES OF MAISIE HITCHINS

The Case of the
Stolen Sixpence

written by Holly Webb
illustrated by Marion Lindsay

Houghton Mifflin Harcourt | Boston New York

31 Albion Street, London

Attic:

Maisie's grandmother and Sarah-Ann the maid

Third floor:

Miss Lane's rooms

Second floor:

Madame Lorimer's rooms

First floor:

Professor Tobin's rooms

Ground floor:

Entrance hall, sitting room and dining room

Basement:

Maisie's room, kitchen and yard entrance

Chapter One

Maisie Hitchins watched, open-mouthed,
as the famous detective Gilbert Carrington
came rushing down the front steps of his
lodging house, hauling on his coat as he ran.
His faithful assistant, Major Edward Lamb,
galloped after him, clutching both their hats,
and they sprang into a cab and rattled away.

Maisie stared after the hansom cab and
sighed heavily. Where could they be going?

It was bound to be somewhere exciting. Chasing jewel thieves, perhaps? Only yesterday, Gran's paper had said that they were on the trail of the Larradine Rubies at last. The newspaper article confidently expected the hunt to take them to India, possibly by way of Paris, or even Madrid. It had sounded wonderful. *Just imagine,* Maisie thought, *following footprints, spotting clues, trailing culprits* . . .

The dust cast up by the cab horse's hooves settled slowly back onto the road, and Maisie set off again. Gran would be waiting for the fish she needed to cook for the lodgers' supper. Maisie's grandmother ran a boarding house, and she spent all her time running around after the fussy lodgers. Maisie scuffed her boots along the pavement sadly. The fish smelled, and it was oozing out of its soggy paper parcel. She was almost certain that Gilbert Carrington never ate fish. He probably instructed his landlady never even to serve it. Certainly not in a parsley sauce, which Maisie really hated. Just because Madame Lorimer, who lived on the second floor of the boarding house, happened to have a fancy for fish, now Maisie would have to have it for her supper as well.

Still. If she hadn't had to run out and fetch the fish, she'd never have seen Gilbert Carrington, Maisie admitted to herself, cheering up a little. Perhaps he'd been on his way to Scotland Yard? Perhaps he'd solved the mystery of the rubies already?

Maisie dawdled along, swinging the basket and daydreaming. If she walked along Laurence Road where Gilbert Carrington lived whenever she was sent out on errands, surely sooner or later she'd meet someone on their way to consult the great detective? It was lucky that he lived so close to her grandmother's lodging house, on Albion Street. If only she could manage to run into one of his clients first, and deduce something amazing. Then she might be able to help him solve a mystery.

Maisie smiled to herself as she imagined the great man pacing up and down his rooms. He probably had all sorts of peculiar things on the walls, things that he'd picked up on his adventures. Strange African spears, sets of handcuffs, amazing jewels that people had given him after he'd rescued them . . . treasure maps . . . Carrington would be smoking his pipe—he was quite often drawn with it in the newspaper cartoons, so

Maisie knew he had one. She had borrowed a pipe once, from the young man who had the third-floor back bedroom, but trying to smoke it had made her sick. And the young man hadn't paid his rent, so she hadn't had a chance to try again. She wasn't sure it was strictly necessary to smoke a pipe to be a great detective, anyway, though it would have helped her look the part.

"Edward," he would groan. "I just don't see it. Something's missing. Some vital

clue . . ." And Maisie would step in, just then, and tell him what it was.

Because Carrington could always be having an off day, Maisie reasoned. It would only take him having a cold, after all. With a blocked-up nose, the great detective wouldn't be able to smell a thing, and smells could be vital.

If she had a cold right now, she wouldn't be able to smell this disgusting fish.

Maisie drew aside politely for an elderly lady in a smart black silk dress and an enormous bonnet to walk past. She tried to look at her as Gilbert Carrington would—every bit of her.

The old lady looked exactly as she ought to, unfortunately. No odd color in her cheeks. No strange jewelry. But Maisie could pretend, just for practice.

Another whiff of fish from the basket reminded her of smells. She ought to check for that. Perhaps the old lady smelled of . . . Maisie frowned to herself, as she tried to think what it could be. It would have to be something unusual, and noticeable . . .

She sniffed thoughtfully. There was actually an odd smell. She just couldn't quite work out what it was.

Aniseed! Maisie glanced over her shoulder in surprise. Of course, the old lady had probably just been eating aniseed balls, but she didn't look like an aniseed ball eater. They were a child's sort of sweet. Surely such a proper-looking person should smell of the usual old lady things. Like violet bonbons, and lavendery lace.

Maisie gave a blissful little shiver. Perhaps the old lady was really a murderess, and she'd used essence of aniseed to confuse a watchdog at her victim's house. Everyone knew that dogs loved aniseed.

Maisie took a few quick steps back down the road after the old lady, who glided on, her black silk dress whispering over the paving slabs. She didn't look like a murderess, but one never knew, after all. Maisie caught her breath, wondering if there was a weapon in the delicate little black reticule she was carrying. She felt in her pocket for her notebook, and the stub of a pencil. She might need to write down her observations . . .

The old lady seemed to sense that she was being followed, and she turned back to glare at Maisie through a pair of gold-rimmed pince-nez spectacles that she had drawn out of her little black bag. It was a particularly freezing glare, and Maisie wilted. She was almost certain that there wasn't room for a dagger or a pistol in the black bag, though. She scuttled away around the corner of the street, cursing herself for being careless and being seen. This detective thing was difficult. Gilbert Carrington would never have let himself be spotted.

Maisie was feeling so ashamed of herself and her dreadful attempts at detection that she almost missed the sack. She had noticed it, of course, as she went past the alley. She was a noticing sort of person. That was what had made her so sure she would make a good detective, if only she was given the chance. At home, all she ever got to do was find Madame Lorimer's knitting, and it was almost always underneath the cushions on the sofa. It was simply a case of following the trail of cake crumbs to work out where the old lady had been sitting last.

There was much more opportunity for detecting out on the streets. But Maisie had been glared at so thoroughly that all she wanted to do was hurry back home and give Gran the basket of fish.

You're a coward, Maisie Hitchins, she told

herself. *What if she really was a murderess? One cross look and you run off like a startled hen.*

Oh well . . . If she was lucky, Gran would be in a good mood (if all the lodgers had paid their rent on time, and no one had complained about a dusty room, or the maid, Sarah-Ann, banging the fire irons). Maisie might even get away with being just a little late. She couldn't really have watched for that long on Laurence Road, could she? But the afternoon sunlight was definitely fading. She hurried past the pile of rubbish in the mouth of the little alleyway leading down to the muddy edge of the canal, and saw the low sun glittering on the water.

Something made her stop and turn back. Why *was* there a sack on the pile of rubbish? It was a perfectly good sack, no rips or holes. It was tied up with a bit of old string, and that was odd, too. Who would bother tying up the top of a sack, just to throw it away? And the sack was dripping wet. That was what had made her turn back, Maisie decided, feeling rather pleased with herself. She must have noticed it without realizing.

Either the sack had been in the canal, or there was something wet inside the sack that was leaking. Or possibly both.

Maisie had been really hoping there was a bloodstained dagger in that old lady's little black reticule, so it was odd that she found herself unwilling to undo the sack and discover what was dripping out of it. A real detective wouldn't hesitate, she told herself crossly, stopping at the mouth of the alley. But what if it *was* a dagger? Or even worse, whatever the dagger had been used on?

One did hear awful stories sometimes, about bits of people left lying around. Gilbert Carrington had managed to solve a murder once just from an ear sent by the penny post in a small brown paper parcel. She shuddered.

It was then that the sack wriggled and let out a despairing whimper.

Maisie gasped, dropped the fish basket, and began to struggle with the damp string at once. There was an animal in there—a dog, she guessed. "Did someone drop you in the canal?" she whispered, her red curls getting in her eyes as she tore at the knots. "I hope you don't bite, although I wouldn't blame you if you did. How long have you been in here?" She dragged the string away at last, and gently folded back the top of the sack.

Looking out at her was a small, grubby, grayish-white face, with brown ears and dark, dark brown eyes. A puppy! Both of the ears were laid anxiously flat against his head, and he stared at Maisie as though he thought she was going to shout at him.

"Are you hurt?" Maisie asked worriedly,

wondering why he didn't jump out of the sack and run away. She'd expected him to disappear as soon as she'd set him free. "Maybe you're just too scared to go past me . . ." she murmured, stepping back a little.

The puppy twitched his shoulders and shook himself free, stepping carefully out of the folds of sacking. Then he hurried over to Maisie and sat down next to her boots.

"Go home!" Maisie told him. Then she sighed, shaking her head. "Of course, you can't—that was stupid. You probably don't have one. But you can't come home with me, you know. Gran won't have a dog in the house. They're too dirty and muddy. She wouldn't even have a cat—she says animals make dust."

The dog simply stared up at her and didn't move. Maisie knew that she ought to

shoo him away, but she couldn't. He seemed
to have decided that he was hers now, and
someone had clearly already tried to drown
the poor little creature. If she didn't take
him home with her, she couldn't see such a
small, bedraggled dog lasting more than a
day or so on the London streets. Someone
would turn him into sausages if he walked
down the wrong alleyway.

"Gran isn't going to be happy if I bring
you home," she muttered. "You'll have to
hide."

The dog shook his ears, as if he was
trying to get the last of the water out.

"Yes, and I hate to say it, but you do
smell rather. You might have to have a bath."
Maisie sighed. "Under the scullery pump,
maybe. I can't see me smuggling you into
the lodgers' bathroom. Someone would

see us, for sure." She crouched down and reached out a hand to rub the little dog's ears. He closed his eyes so blissfully when Maisie scratched them that she realized he probably had fleas.

Just how did you get out of the canal? Maisie wondered as she scooped up the fish basket and set off down the road again, the dog trotting next to her, so close that his thin little tail slapped against her boots. "I suppose it was quite a big sack. You must have scrabbled about inside it enough to stay afloat, and then got yourself washed up. If that's what happened, you were very lucky."

The dog glanced up at her brightly, as though to say that he made his own luck, and Maisie laughed. Now that he was drying out a bit, she noticed one of his ears was at a very funny angle, set a little sideways, like a daring, rakish sort of hat. He was very sweet, even if he was dirty. How could someone have tried to drown him?

"I suppose," Maisie said thoughtfully, "that all great detectives have a faithful companion, like Gilbert Carrington has Major Edward Lamb. He's supposed to be awfully good in a fight. He has a swordstick, according to the *Morning Post,* and he's saved Gilbert Carrington's life at least twice. Although of course Mr. Carrington has saved him hundreds of times." She looked down at the dog, who was sniffing at something disgusting in the gutter. "Perhaps you'll save me one day," she said. "You could be my companion. I think I'll call you Eddie . . ."

Chapter Two

"Maisie! Maisie!"

Maisie turned around, trying to see
who was calling her. Whoever it was, they
were being very quiet and polite about it.
Eventually, she spotted a girl in a beautiful
blue and white sailor dress, standing on the
front steps of a house across the street.

"Alice!"

Alice was the daughter of a very rich

shipping merchant, and her mother had died when Alice was a baby. Her father fussed over her all the time, and he had engaged a horribly prim and proper governess, Miss Sidebotham, who was supposed to be turning Alice into a perfect young lady.

Maisie had met Alice when she came to the lodging house for lessons in French conversation with Madame Lorimer. Luckily for the girls, although Madame Lorimer was very good at French conversation, she always fell asleep in the afternoons, so Alice and Maisie were usually able to sneak away and chat. Maisie had to make sure she wasn't around when Miss Sidebotham came to collect Alice, though. She wouldn't have thought the landlady's granddaughter was a suitable friend for her dear little Alice. Plus Maisie couldn't help sniggering whenever the governess's name was mentioned. It sounded exactly like Sidebottom, and Miss Sidebotham's rear end was rather enormous.

Maisie beamed at Alice. She darted across the road to see her friend and pretended she didn't hear the errand boy on the bicycle shouting at her. He really hadn't had to swerve all that much, and it was rare that she got an extra chance to talk to Alice. They had tried sending each other messages in a rather clever code. They'd based it on words in Mr. Dickens's *Oliver Twist*, which a long-ago lodger had left behind at Albion Street. Alice's father had given her a copy as a birthday present, so they had a book each. But it didn't work very well. Alice wasn't often able to post her messages through Maisie's door, for a start. When she did manage it, Gran always wanted to know what the strange strings of words meant, which hardly made them feel secret.

"You've got a dog! You're so lucky . . ." Alice crouched down and crooned lovingly at Eddie, who peeped shyly at her around Maisie's ankles. "He's a darling. Oh, I wish Father and Miss Sidebotham would let me have a dog."

Maisie nodded understandingly. The chances of Alice being allowed a dog were very slim. Her father was so fussy.

"He isn't really mine," Maisie admitted. "Although I suppose he doesn't belong to anyone else. I found him . . ." She glanced anxiously at Alice, who was so coddled that she'd probably never heard of puppies being drowned before. "Someone threw him in the canal. In a sack."

"Who?" Alice squeaked, looking outraged.

Eddie ducked back worriedly behind Maisie's legs.

"Oh, I'm sorry, darling dog. Maisie, who would do such a horrible thing?"

Maisie sighed. "Lots of people, Alice. But it *is* awful. I couldn't leave him, and now I'm

going to have to sneak him past Gran and try to keep him a secret. It's very lucky that my room is out of everybody else's way."

Mrs. Hitchins's lodging house was very popular, due to her excellent meals and reasonable rates, so the apartments on the main floors were almost always let. The family fitted themselves into the odd little bits of the house that weren't rented out. Sarah-Ann, the maid, and Maisie's gran slept up in the attic, and Gran had a neat little sitting room on the ground floor. Now that Maisie was twelve, she had her own tiny room at the back of the scullery in the basement. Although it was tiny, and really meant for keeping brooms and buckets in, Maisie didn't mind at all. The room led out onto the narrow passage to the kitchen, and from the passage she could go up a few steps and straight out into the little yard at the back of the house. It meant Maisie could get in and out without too many people noticing. It was also perfect for smuggling in a dog.

"Alice, I'd better go. I was only sent out to fetch the fish for Gran's lodgers, and she'll be desperate for it by now. It's ever so late. Have you got French conversation on Friday?"

Alice nodded. *"Au revoir,* Maisie," she giggled. *"Au revoir, petit chien."* Then, as Maisie turned to go, she added seriously, "Maisie, you ought to find out who tried to drown him. It's a mystery, so you could do your detecting. You love detecting! Someone who'd do that to a dear little dog might do anything!"

Maisie nodded, and clicked her fingers.

Eddie trotted after her at once, down the darkening street and around a couple more corners, until they came to the neat, green-painted gate that led into the yard at the back of 31 Albion Street. "You have to be very quiet!" she told Eddie sternly, and she was pleased to see that he tucked his thin little tail neatly between his legs and pricked up his funny ear as though he was waiting for instructions.

"Good boy," Maisie whispered. "Come on." She opened the gate and peered around it to see if anyone was looking out of the scullery window. They would only see her feet, as the scullery was lower than the yard, but they couldn't miss seeing small white paws, too.

Not wanting to take any chances, Maisie crouched down and picked the little dog up,

tucking him under the floral cape she was wearing crossed over her jacket. Gran had a horror of the fog getting to her chest, and now that it was late autumn, she wouldn't let Maisie out of the house without at least five layers of clothes. Luckily, Eddie was small enough and the muffler large enough that it just about hid him. "I could have put you in the basket with the fish," she muttered. "But that would be cruel—the smell's bad enough for me, let alone a dog."

She hurried down the steps into the scullery passage and into her tiny bedroom, where she pulled the thick woolen blanket off the end of her bed and folded it up into a cushion for Eddie. "Stay there," she told him, wriggling out of her muffler and putting it down on the cushion with the small dog still wrapped in it. "Stay!"

Eddie stared back at her, his bright black eyes shining out of the nest of wool, and Maisie saw how nicely he curled up, and how much cozier her bare little room looked with a dog in it. She just *had* to keep him. Whatever Gran said.

"I'll find you something to eat in a minute," she told him, shutting the door firmly behind her.

She was expecting her grandmother to be in the kitchen, probably furious with her for being so late, but the kitchen and scullery were both empty, and Maisie could hear some sort of commotion going on above stairs. She took the fish out of the basket, left it on the kitchen table, and hurried up to investigate.

Gran and Sarah-Ann were standing in the hallway, watching rather helplessly as two men carried in neat wooden packing crates and huge cloth bundles, glass cases, and even a parrot in a gilded dome of a cage.

"Oh . . . a parrot . . ." Gran said faintly. "I'm really not sure I can allow . . ."

Maisie came further up the stairs and saw that supervising the two men was a small,

thin figure wrapped in an enormous tweed overcoat, with an absurd tweed hat with earflaps. "Oh, my dear lady, Jasper is most beautifully trained, I do assure you. Very quiet. Very polite. No bad language."

"I should hope not," Gran said.

"Perhaps the young lady would like to

earn a shilling or two looking after his cage," the old man suggested, peering at Maisie with dark eyes that glittered under the bushiest eyebrows she had ever seen.

Maisie nodded eagerly. If she had some extra money, she could buy scraps for Eddie. She had been wondering how she'd manage to feed him without sneaking food from the kitchen all the time. It was hard enough for Gran to make ends meet without Maisie feeding a dog, too. "Of course, sir," she said, bobbing a little curtsey. She knew who he was now. She had forgotten that Gran had told her the best rooms, the ones that took the whole of the first floor, were let again. They had been taken by an old gentleman who had come recommended by Madame Lorimer. He had been a friend of the French lady's husband, many years ago, and he was some sort of professor. Looking at his boxes and bundles of strange stuff, Maisie couldn't imagine what he professed in.

"This is Professor Tobin, Maisie," Gran said with a sigh. She looked as though she wasn't sure about her new lodger at all, but Maisie thought he might be rather fun. A lot more interesting than the bad-tempered old lady who'd had the rooms before, anyway. And Gran would be pleased once all the mess of his boxes was out of the hallway. Now that all the rooms were let except for those on the ground floor, which had most of the noise from the road, it would mean the household expenses weren't so dear. Madame Lorimer and Miss Lottie Lane, the actress who had the third-floor rooms now, didn't pay as much as whoever took the first floor. Their rooms were nice, but not as smart, and the staircases needed painting. The first-floor apartments were much bigger than the rooms higher up the house, and well furnished, with an almost-new crimson damask wallpaper, so they brought in most of the money.

Maisie hadn't been at all sure about bringing home a puppy. She had never owned one before, and she didn't know an awful lot about them. She hadn't expected Eddie to be so friendly, or so much fun to watch. But by the next morning, she was wondering how she had gotten along without a dog for so long. She had found a broken old comb that Miss Lane had given her, and with it combed through Eddie's coat. He did have fleas, but not very many, and she knew how to catch them by squashing them into a bar of soap. Miss Lane had taught her that trick as well—she said that theaters weren't called fleapits for nothing.

Maisie hadn't had the heart to try to wash him properly under the scullery pump—what if it reminded him of the canal? So she'd taken a bucket of water and some rags and done her best to sponge him down. He didn't smell all that bad now, which was a relief, as he hadn't stayed on his cushion for long once she went to bed—he had scrabbled and wriggled his way up onto her feet and then squashed himself blissfully between Maisie and the wall. He snored. Luckily, Gran always said that Maisie did too, so hopefully anyone who heard him would just think that Maisie had a cold. That wouldn't work if he started to bark, though, Maisie thought, as she sat up in bed stroking him the next morning. It was lucky that he seemed to be a very calm, quiet sort of dog. So far . . .

Lovely though it was to have a dog to sleep on her bed, Maisie still had the problem of feeding him. She had saved a piece of her fish the night before (not much of a hardship), but Eddie was clearly hungry again this morning. He stared up at her with round, hopeful eyes that made her feel terribly guilty.

"I'm sorry. There isn't much. I'll try to save you some of my breakfast, but it'll be porridge, and I'm not sure how I can get it to you. I can hardly wrap it in my handkerchief, can I?"

Eddie put one small paw on her knee and stared up at her adoringly.

Maisie sighed. "All right. I'll manage somehow. Oh, Gran's calling. I'll be back soon."

But she wasn't. There was breakfast, and then there were errands, and polishing, and dusting the new gentleman's rooms, with strict instructions from Gran not to touch anything. Maisie wasn't sure how she was supposed to dust without touching things — just flap the duster around? It was interesting, though, and Professor Tobin didn't seem to mind her touching things in the slightest. In fact, he kept getting up from his desk to show them to her properly. He had rather a lot of stuffed animals, which he explained he was studying, for his book. He tried to explain what the book was about, but it was very complicated and seemed to be all to do with how much fur creatures had, and people having once had fur too,

which couldn't be right, could it?

By the time Maisie got back downstairs

it was past ten, and she knew that Eddie would be starving. She hadn't heard any barking from upstairs, but what if he started whining, or scratching at the door?

"Maisie!" Her grandmother was standing in front of Maisie's door as she came into the scullery. "Whatever is making that noise in your room? I thought it was you, with the most dreadful toothache!" As she spoke, she flung open the bedroom door, and Eddie burst out, and raced through the scullery and into the kitchen, where Sarah-Ann was telling the butcher's boy that he'd brought the wrong thing again.

"It's all there, just what was on the order! Don't you go blaming me if the missus has changed her mind. Hey!" The boy wheeled around as Eddie scrambled over his feet, up the steps, and out into the yard. "Didn't know you had a dog."

"We do not," Gran snapped. "That creature does not belong here."

There was a crash from the yard, and the butcher's boy said something that made Gran put her hands over Maisie's ears. Then he ran up the steps.

Maisie struggled away from Gran and dashed after him. The bicycle, with its huge basket on the front for carrying the deliveries, had fallen over (or been pulled) and Eddie was half in, half out of the basket, letting out joyful little whines as he smelled bacon and kidneys and someone's joint of beef.

"Get out of it!" yelled the butcher's boy, and Eddie jumped out of the basket, trailing a string of plump pink sausages. He raced across the yard, the sausages bouncing behind him, and disappeared out of the open gate.

Maisie ran after him, wondering worriedly how much it would cost to replace the sausages — she didn't think the butcher's boy would want them back now, even if she could get them off Eddie.

The butcher's boy was chasing them too, she realized as she darted out of the gate, but he was slowed down by picking up the bicycle and the scattered parcels from the basket. He looked furious. Maisie hurried after Eddie. She had to get to him before that boy did.

Out in the street, several people had clearly just turned to watch Eddie scamper past, and Maisie could see a little white shape approaching Callary Lane.

There seemed to be fewer sausages than before—she was rather impressed that Eddie could eat and run at the same time.

"Come back here, you little rat!" the butcher's boy yelled, pelting out of the yard on his bike and wobbling off in pursuit. He hadn't loaded the basket very well and he was off-balance, which slowed him down.

Maisie took a deep breath and ran as fast as she could, calling, "Eddie! Eddie!"

He'd been called Eddie for less than a day, she realized sadly. He wasn't likely to listen, not with all the carts and carriages rumbling past and that boy yelling after him too.

Eddie was in the middle of Callary Lane now, and Maisie could see a smart carriage coming down the road at a swift pace. "Eddie!" she screamed. "Here!"

Eddie turned back, still trailing sausages, and dithered in the middle of the road. The

coachman yelled something that Maisie thought was probably even ruder than the words the butcher's boy had said, and swerved sharply to the side of the road, nearly running down a flower stall. Eddie shot out of the road and back to Maisie, so shocked by the huge black carriage bearing down on him that he actually dropped the sausages.

Maisie scooped him up and raced away around a corner before the coachman could disentangle himself from some roses and catch her. But she'd forgotten about the butcher's boy, who came lumbering after her on his bicycle, shouting. "What about the sausages, you little thief!"

"Sssshhhh!" Maisie hissed at him. "They'll catch us. Eddie scratched the carriage's paintwork, and there were dozens of roses all over the street. Be quiet, can't you?"

"They oughter catch you!" the boy snapped back. "That dog's a menace. And you owe me sixpence for the sausages. And I'm late for my round now. I'll catch it off the old man."

"I'll pay you back, I promise," Maisie sighed, thinking that the parrot's cage was going to have to get cleaned out ever such a lot. "Tell the butcher to put the sausages on Gran's account, and I'll make it up to her. Can't you just tell him what happened?"

"What? That I let a dog the size of a mouse tip my bike over and steal half the delivery?" the boy sighed. "Old Harrowby's never going to believe that. Honestly, you're a nuisance, Maisie Hitchins."

Maisie Hitchins? How did he know her name? Maisie blinked and stared at him under his cap. Then she realized. She knew him. She felt quite cross with herself—a detective ought never to forget a face. The boy's name was George, and she had been to the same school as he had. George had left once he was ten, a couple of years before Maisie had to leave to help Gran in the lodgings. And, of course, he had been taught in the boys' class. But Maisie remembered his little sister, Lucy. George had brought her to school. They lived a few streets away, quite close to the butcher's shop.

Maisie looked at him hopefully. "You could say Eddie was bigger," she said. "A wolfhound, perhaps? There's a wolfhound lives on Laurence Road. I've seen it—it's huge. Please, George?"

"Oh, all right then," George said, sighing and rolling his eyes. "But from now on you'd better keep that little horror quiet!"

Chapter Three

Maisie was so glad to have found Eddie, unsquashed and not thrown back into the canal by furious coachmen or butcher's boys, that she hurried back home with him in her arms. He kept wriggling and licking her nose.

It wasn't until she reached the alley that ran along the back of the houses on Albion

Street and saw her grandmother looking out the gate that she remembered. Her secret was out. Gran had seen Eddie and she knew that he'd been in Maisie's room.

Maisie slowed to a walk. Gran didn't like dogs. She thought they were messy and troublesome. (Based on this morning, she was right, but then she didn't know how it felt to have a warm, solid lump of dog curled up beside you in bed.)

Eddie twisted in her arms as though he could feel that something was wrong.

"Don't worry," Maisie murmured to him. "I'll persuade her. Somehow."

Her grandmother was frowning, and she had her arms folded across her dark brown dress in a way that Maisie knew wasn't a good sign.

"Exactly what was that animal doing in your room?" she snapped as Maisie trailed up to her. "Where did you get him from?"

"I found him, Gran. I rescued him out of a sack. Someone had tried to drown him." Maisie hugged the puppy tightly. It still made her shiver to think of it.

"I'm not surprised. Dirty little thing."

"Oh, Gran, he isn't! I washed him, and he's so good."

"Good! He's a disgrace! I shouldn't think Harrowby's will ever deliver here again! Where am I to get the meat from now, Maisie?"

Maisie shook her head. "They will! I spoke to the boy, Gran. He'll put the sausages on our account. I'll earn the money from Professor Tobin to pay you for them, and I'll pay for all Eddie's food, I promise. It was only that he was hungry. He'd been shut up all morning with nothing to eat. He'll be a good guard dog, Gran. And a ratter. You're always complaining about the horrible big rats."

"A guard dog?" Gran shook her head in disbelief. "Maisie, he's tiny. He couldn't guard a cup of tea! And how can he catch rats when most of them are bigger than he is? I don't have money to throw away feeding a dog, Maisie. You have to put him right back where you found him."

"I can't!" Maisie wailed. "I found him by the canal. He can't go back there. He'll grow ever so much bigger — he's only a puppy now. He'll make a good ratter, I promise."

Her grandmother snorted crossly. "Lot of nonsense. And he isn't growing bigger on the scraps from my kitchen." She glared at Eddie, and he stared back at her with big, mournful eyes. "You can keep him until tomorrow. But you have to look for a new home for him. And he stays in the yard, Maisie, not in the house!"

Maisie sat on an upturned box in the yard, watching Eddie darting about. Really, she ought to be helping Sarah-Ann with the washing-up from lunch, but the young maid had hustled her out of the scullery. She said that Maisie was worse than useless today and she'd be better off outside. Sarah-Ann felt sorry for her, Maisie realized, sorry that Gran was making her get rid of Eddie.

Eddie was chasing leaves now, pouncing on them as they swirled in the wind, and growling at them furiously. Maisie couldn't help giggling at him even though she was worried; he was so funny.

What was she going to do? How could she find him another home by tomorrow? Maisie was quite sure that Gran meant what she said.

"Maybe Alice could hide you for a bit," she murmured. But Alice's house was so full of servants, and her governess had eyes in the back of her head. It wasn't likely.

Maisie sighed and gazed helplessly around the yard. It was chilly, sitting out here, and it was going to be even chillier tonight. She'd have to make up a little bed for Eddie in the coal bunker. Or maybe in the outhouse—though if Gran or Sarah-Ann had a call of nature in the night, that might be a problem. And the smell might put Eddie off, too.

A movement in one of the upstairs windows caught her eye—it was Professor Tobin on the first floor. Maisie squinted at the window uncertainly. Was he waving at her? And now he was putting a finger to his lips . . .

The professor turned away for a moment, then he lifted the sash window and started to lower something—something brown and furry.

"Untie it!" the professor hissed as the brown thing came swiftly down, just missing the little window from the kitchen.

Maisie blinked, then did as she was told. It was one of his stuffed creatures, she realized. She thought this one was called a wombat—she remembered it, because it had sounded so funny. She undid the string and the professor quickly hauled it back up. "Put it in the middle of the yard!" he called quietly.

Maisie did as she was told, wondering if this was some sort of experiment. Eddie came trotting over—the wombat was about the same size as he was, and he stared into its glass eyes, looking very confused.

"Goodness me!" the professor bawled, so loudly that Maisie jumped, and Eddie let out a little yip of fright. "Oh, good heavens! Mrs. Hitchins! Mrs. Hitchins!"

Then he beamed hugely at Maisie and disappeared from the window. She could hear him as he hurried down the stairs.

"Whatever is it!" someone exclaimed, and then there was a clatter of boots as the professor erupted into the kitchen, still shouting.

"Did you see it? My goodness! Out in the yard! The most enormous rat I've ever seen! Thank goodness you've had the sense to purchase a terrier, Mrs. Hitchins. He'll deal with the beasts. My specimens, you know! I can't have them nibbled. I thought I heard some scratching behind the skirting boards last night." The professor appeared at the door to the yard and made anxious flapping gestures at Maisie, who was gaping at him. He was pointing at the wombat.

It did look quite like a rat . . .

"Good boy!" Maisie squeaked. "Oh, good boy, Eddie! I think he's got it, Professor. It, er, it isn't moving anymore . . ." She stuffed her hand into her mouth so as not to laugh.

"Excellent, excellent. Shall I dispose of the nasty creature, Mrs. Hitchins? You ladies don't want to be dealing with that." He darted forward as Gran and Sarah-Ann crowded behind him, and threw an old piece of sacking over the wombat. He gathered it up, and strolled toward the yard gate. He stopped to pat Eddie's head, and drooped one eyelid in a slow wink at Maisie. "What a clever little dog you are. A wonderful ratter. Well done, Mrs. Hitchins."

Gran and Sarah-Ann and Maisie stared after him, and then looked down at the little white dog, now sitting sweetly at their feet.

"I suppose we'll have to keep him then,"

Gran sighed, looking down at Eddie. "If the professor likes him. But not in the kitchen, Maisie. Not ever."

"Unless there's a rat, Mrs. Hitchins, ma'am," Sarah-Ann said nervously. "Mice I can chase out with the broom, I don't mind that. But that rat was a monster! Did you see its teeth? It could have had your finger off!"

"Don't be silly," Gran snapped, but she didn't sound as sharp as usual. Maisie was quite sure Gran hated rats too.

"I'm sure just having Eddie close will scare them away," Maisie said hopefully. It might be true . . . She had seen rats in the yard, several times, though none of them had been wombat-sized.

Gran glared at Eddie. "There's a ham bone in the pantry," she said, rather crossly. "You'd better fetch it for him, Maisie. And that chipped pie dish — he can have that for a water bowl. But if there's any mess, out he'll go!"

"Yes, Gran!" Maisie threw her arms around her gran's spotless white apron and hugged her tightly. "He'll be a little angel. I promise."

Chapter Four

The next morning, Eddie sniffed around
in the yard while Maisie did her work
upstairs. Once her gran was out doing the
shopping, Maisie did sneak him into the
kitchen and Sarah-Ann fed him some bacon
rind. Since the professor's amazing rat trick,
Sarah-Ann would have given Eddie roast
swan if she could have found any. They
hustled him quickly back out into Maisie's

room when they heard Gran coming back.

"Stay there, now," Maisie told him. "I've got to wash the breakfast dishes. Piles and piles of them. The professor does like his breakfast. Then maybe we can slip out for a walk later on. We need to go back to the alley where I found you, don't we? Alice is right. You're a mystery, my first proper case. I have to find out who tried to get rid of you like that."

Eddie began to bark sharply, and at first Maisie thought he'd understood what she'd said. But then she heard the click of the yard gate. She smiled down at him, frisking back and forth in front of the back door. "You see, I knew you'd be a good guard dog," she told him, going to open the door.

The pale, scrawny boy who stood there was a couple of years older than she was. He was wearing a scruffy waistcoat, and a familiar-looking greasy apron. "Got yer meat delivery," he told her, handing her a parcel wrapped in waxed paper.

"But . . ." Maisie glanced at the bicycle he'd propped against the wall. It was a different boy. Not George. Had Gran changed butchers after all? Had the butcher kicked up a fuss about those sausages? But Gran hadn't said anything about it, and the sign on the bicycle still said Harrowby's Finest Meat Pies. "What happened to the other boy?" she asked.

The boy sneered. "Sweet on him, was yer? Get off, nasty little beggar." He aimed a kick at Eddie, who was sniffing around his boots.

"Don't do that!" Maisie went pink. "And I certainly wasn't sweet on George! I just wondered why it was you instead."

He shrugged. "George got the boot. He'd been stealing, the old man said. Got his fingers in the cash box. If I see George, I'll tell him you was asking after him." He climbed back on the bicycle and rode unsteadily away, as though he wasn't used to it.

Maisie stared after him, frowning.

Stealing? George? Maisie was surprised. It seemed unlikely from what she knew of him. She stared after the other boy. He was a lot less polite than George (or than George was when a dog hadn't just stolen a string of sausages from him, anyway). And he didn't ride a bike nearly as well. She didn't think he'd be as popular with the houses he delivered to. George had always said *Miss* and *Madam*, and pulled at the peak of his cap as he said goodbye—like a salute.

And with her detective hat on, there was something else bothering Maisie—the way George had chased after Eddie and those sausages didn't feel right. If he was a thief, surely he wouldn't have been all that bothered? And he hadn't wanted to lie to Mr. Harrowby, either . . .

Maisie's eyes widened. What if Mr.

Harrowby hadn't believed George about the dog? George had been worried that he wouldn't. And then he'd given him the sack, because he thought George had taken the sausages!

If that was what had happened, she and Eddie had lost him his job!

"We'll have to go and find him," Maisie murmured. "And then I'll go back to Harrowby's with him and say it was all my fault. Then Mr. Harrowby will have to give him his job back, won't he?" She looked anxiously down at Eddie, who twitched his funny ear at her. "You are a nuisance . . . But I do love you," she added hurriedly.

Maisie had a reasonable idea where George lived, from talking to his sister Lucy at school. She was sure she could find their lodgings.

Glancing quickly over her shoulder to see if anyone was around, Maisie darted back into her room to fetch her jacket, and then hurried out into the yard, with Eddie following after her, dragging his ham bone.

Maisie sighed. "You can't bring that. No."

Eddie stared up at her. He had never had a bone of his own before, Maisie supposed. He had tried to lift it onto her bed last night, and he'd given her a very reproachful look when she hadn't helped him. In the end he'd slept with his nose over the edge of the bed so as to be as near to it as possible.

Now he sat down in the middle of the yard, next to the bone, and looked from Maisie to the bone and back again, his ears twitching anxiously.

"You can stay here with it," Maisie suggested, going to open the yard gate. "But

I've got to go. If Gran catches me she'll have me polishing the banisters or something."

Eddie frantically dragged the bone behind the coal bunker and dashed after her. Maisie smiled to herself. It was nice to know that she was slightly more important than a bone.

They set off toward the busier streets,

heading past the butcher's shop (Maisie picked Eddie up here), and then into the lanes behind (where she put him back down). Maisie was concentrating so hard on remembering where George lived that she almost missed it when George himself walked past her. She only realized when Eddie came to a stop and turned to growl at someone.

"Hey!" She turned back, catching his sleeve.

George stopped and sighed. "You again. And the sausage dog."

Maisie stared at him anxiously. He looked grayish, and miserable. Even his fair hair seemed to have lost its color, and his clothes looked somehow shabbier already. "I was actually looking for you," she explained. "Did he sack you because of the sausages?

Mr. Harrowby, I mean. I'm so sorry. I'll go and tell him it was all my fault. I never meant for you to lose your job!"

George shook his head. "It wasn't that. I don't think it helped much, but he sacked me because there was money missing from the cash box. Odd bits. Just a shilling or so, here and there. He reckoned it had to be someone who works in the shop, so he marked some of the money in the cash box."

Maisie blinked admiringly. That was the sort of clever thing that Gilbert Carrington would do to catch a thief. "How?" she asked eagerly.

George looked at her in surprise. "How what?"

"How did he mark it?" asked Maisie.

"Paint," said George. "Instead of taking all the money out of the cash box one night, he marked some of the coins with a little bit of yellow paint, and put them back as the change for the next day. Then a couple of days later, he lined us all up, and made us turn out our pockets—me, Sally, who takes the money and writes up the ledgers, and both of the assistants, one of them who's his own nephew, even."

Maisie frowned. "But I don't understand. You hadn't stolen the money, so how come you got sacked?" Then she went red. "I suppose . . . you didn't actually steal it, did you?"

"No!" George shouted, loudly enough that people turned to look, and Eddie darted worriedly behind Maisie's ankles.

"I didn't think you had," Maisie assured him. "I just don't see how you got the sack if you didn't have the marked money."

George rubbed the toe of his scruffy boot in the dust. "I did have it," he admitted. "Just one sixpence." He glanced up at Maisie, his eyes pleading. "I found it! It was in the yard, under some straw! Whoever it was who took the money must have dropped it, or maybe they hid all the money there for a bit? All I did was pick it up," he added. "It isn't fair."

"I don't suppose Mr. Harrowby believed you when you told him that, though," Maisie said.

George made a noise that was half laugh, half grunt. "Not a chance. He said I was a shameless liar and a thief, and he sacked me."

Maisie looked thoughtful. She could see how it looked, but she was sure that George was honest. It wasn't fair. She looked at him hopefully. "We'll just have to find out who really took the money, then," she said. "Who else could it be?"

George shrugged. "I don't see how we can work that out."

"I will," Maisie said firmly. "I'm sure I will. It could have been any one of the people who work in the shop! I don't think much of Mr. Harrowby's judgment—I reckon the new boy's much more likely to be a thief than you. I wouldn't trust him at all. He's rude."

George's eyes widened, and then he seemed to go even grayer. "Got a new boy already, have they? Didn't take them long."

Maisie frowned. "How's your mum going to manage without your wages?"

George straightened up and glared at her. "Mind your own business," he snapped.

"Sorry . . . Don't go!"

But George was already marching away furiously, and Maisie sighed. She shouldn't have said that. But she had a horrible feeling that George's mother and Lucy relied on the money he earned. They really needed it, and if he'd been sacked for stealing, he'd never get another job.

Even though it wasn't her fault he'd been sacked, Maisie still felt responsible. She picked Eddie up and hugged him tightly, watching as George plunged away down the lane.

Now she had two mysteries to solve.

Chapter Five

"Drat it . . ."

"What's wrong, Gran?" Maisie looked around from the potatoes she was peeling. Since Gran had let her keep Eddie, she was trying to be amazingly well behaved. Eddie wasn't, so she had to be.

"Professor Tobin wants a steak and kidney pudding for his dinner. I clean forgot to buy the meat when I went to the butcher's this morning."

Maisie jumped up from the table. "I can go!" She grabbed her jacket from the hook and hurried to the back door.

"Maisie! Wait—you don't know what I want, child," cried Gran. "And you need a basket. Here, I'll write it down. Don't let them give you too much sinew—they're bound to try it on, with it being you instead of me."

Maisie went off with the basket, grinning to herself. She'd been trying to work out how to do some detective work around what was going on at the butcher's shop, so going to buy some steak and kidney was perfect. Gran always did the morning shopping herself, and got most of her purchases sent home by the boys from the grocer and the butcher. She had occasionally tried to take Maisie with her, but Maisie hated shopping so much that they usually ended up quarreling.

Maisie couldn't tell her gran the real reason she wanted to go out. Gran wouldn't approve of detecting at all. She would just think that Maisie was snooping. If Maisie ever became a professional detective like she wanted to, she knew she'd never be allowed to work from Albion Street. Which was sad, because Professor Tobin's rooms on the first floor would make excellent consulting rooms for a detective.

With Eddie trotting in front of her, Maisie wandered on, imagining Gran showing in her clients. "Her Grace the Duchess, Miss Hitchins. Here about the diamonds . . ."

And Maisie would smile and nod, and

ask the duchess to sit down before she told
her that the diamonds had been stolen by
her new lady's maid, who wasn't a lady's
maid at all. They could be found in the
green suitcase under her bed. All of which
Maisie had worked out from the way the
duchess's new shoes clearly pinched her feet.
No real lady's maid would let her mistress go
out in ill-fitting shoes!

Maisie wasn't quite sure how she'd
detected the green suitcase, but she was sure
that she would. After all, by then she would
have had years of practice.

Maisie shook her head firmly.
Concentrate, Maisie Hitchins! she demanded.
She had a real case now. Her first actual
case, with a proper crime and everything. Of
course, Maisie still wanted to know who had
tried to drown Eddie, but not many other

people would call it a crime. This one was different. Even Gran would be impressed if she solved the case of the stolen sixpence.

The new delivery boy shot out of the alleyway that led to the yard at the back of the butcher's as Maisie came up the road. She had to jump back against the wall to keep from getting hit, and Eddie yelped with fright.

"That stupid boy!" Maisie muttered, stroking the puppy's ears. "George might have been a bit rude about you eating the sausages, but he never ran into people. We have to get him his job back."

Harrowby's wasn't the smartest butcher's, but Mrs. Hitchins had always shopped there. She said she didn't want to be sneered at by those smart assistants in the new butcher's up the road, the one that had the plate-glass windows with the gold lettering on. Maisie didn't like either of them. She hated seeing the meat hanging up in the windows, and outside sometimes too. She didn't much like the spongy feel of the damp sawdust on the floor either.

"Stay here, Eddie," she told the puppy, tying the piece of twine she'd fastened on to his new collar to a ring outside. Then she squared her shoulders and marched into the shop. It was quite busy, with the butcher himself talking to a smartly dressed lady and several other shoppers in front of Maisie.

"Serve the young lady, Alfred!" Mr. Harrowby nodded at her eventually, and Maisie wrinkled her nose as she tried to remember the name. Alfred . . . he must be one of the assistants. She had her tiny notebook and a stub of pencil to write down clues in the pocket of her jacket, but she could hardly get them out and start scribbling now.

"Morning, miss." The young assistant leaned over the counter at last, pretending he could hardly see her, and Maisie sighed. It wasn't really that funny being short.

"Pound of your best stewing steak, and my gran says not too much sinew. And three kidneys."

The young man rolled his eyes, but he fetched a knife and started to chop up the meat for her on the big wooden slab.

Maisie wandered along the counter, dodging her way through the other customers, and eyed the big wooden box where the money was kept. It didn't look easy to open without someone seeing. Certainly the customers couldn't get to it, which was something she'd been wondering. But then, if you were putting in the money, perhaps it wouldn't be too hard to palm a few of the coins.

It was stupid to have sacked George,

Maisie thought, frowning to herself. He did the deliveries and the odd jobs. He didn't serve customers and take money. How would he ever be able to steal from the box? The shop seemed very busy — someone would have noticed the delivery boy messing around with the money.

Still, Mr. Harrowby obviously believed he had. And the only way to change his mind was to find the real thief.

"There you are, miss. Taking it yourself, are you? Bit heavy for a young lady like you," Alfred chuckled. "Send it with the delivery boy, if you like!"

Maisie clenched her teeth, and then realized this was a chance to do some investigating. "Is that George, the delivery boy?" she asked innocently. "I was at school with him."

Alfred shook his head. "Nope. New one now, called Reg."

"What happened to George?" Maisie asked aloud.

"Caught stealing," the young man said shortly, glancing around at Mr. Harrowby, who was still smiling and bowing at the smart lady. Perhaps they weren't supposed to talk about it.

"Oh! What did he steal? Meat?" Maisie widened her eyes, and tried to look as though she didn't already know.

"The money kept coming up short at the end of the day, see." Alfred was frowning. "We write it all down in a ledger—Sal does that, mostly, don't you, Sal?" He nodded to the pretty girl sitting at a tall desk behind him, who was putting down the details of Maisie's purchases on Gran's account. "Little bits of money missing, here and there. Never much. Adds up, though. My uncle decided to put a stop to it."

His uncle . . . Maisie reminded herself to write that into her little notebook. George had said that one of the assistants was the butcher's nephew. He wouldn't be likely to steal from family, would he? And she was sure she'd heard Gran mention Mr. Harrowby's nephew before — she'd complained that he wasn't polite enough for someone who was going to own the shop one day.

Maisie eyed Alfred thoughtfully. There was a shiny watch chain looping across his waistcoat, underneath his butcher's apron. And he was growing a mustache with curly ends — it was nearly as big as his uncle's. He didn't look as though he was desperate enough to borrow from the cash box. Unless, of course, he'd bought the watch with stolen money . . .

"But how did he know it was George?" Maisie asked.

Alfred frowned at her. "Ever so interested, aren't you? Because it was, all right? Certainly wasn't me, or Frank, or Sal!"

Frank? He must be the other assistant, Maisie thought to herself. She shrugged. "But he didn't ever seem like a thief when I knew him," she persisted, smiling sweetly as she put the steak and kidney in her basket. And with that, she left the shop.

Both Sally and Alfred were staring after her as she untied Eddie and hurried away, the young man standing at the door of the shop and Sally peering out of the window.

Is that suspicious? Maisie wondered. But it couldn't be both of them, surely . . .

She stopped once she rounded the corner and took a deep, gulping breath. Detecting was harder than she'd thought it would be. People just didn't want to tell you things.

Leaning against the wall, she pulled out her notebook and sucked the end of her pencil thoughtfully.

Not Alfred? she scribbled. *His shop one day, so why steal?* She turned back a page to her list of suspects and crossed him out. She wasn't absolutely certain, but he just didn't seem likely, and she had to start somewhere.

But there hadn't been any other clues at the butcher's, not as far as she could see. Except that everyone who worked there seemed a bit shifty.

One thing was clear. She wasn't going to be able to go back to Harrowby's and ask any more questions. Or not without them complaining to her gran, anyway.

"It's difficult," Alice agreed as they huddled together at the bottom of the second-floor stairs. Alice had Eddie in her lap, and she was running his funny ear through her fingers, which he loved so much, he was actually drooling. Alice had put her handkerchief under him to soak it up. "I wonder if I could go to the butcher's to take a look? Miss Sidebotham is always saying that I'll have to know how to run my own house one day. Perhaps I could get our housekeeper to take me shopping." She sighed. "But I'm not very good at spotting things, Maisie. Not like you."

"I don't think either of us is much use," Maisie sighed. "The thing is, people don't expect girls to be asking questions in shops. I ought to be a nosy old lady, complaining about the bacon fat or something. There's always someone moaning in Harrowby's, and it's usually an old lady."

"You know what you need," a voice came from behind them, and both Maisie and

Alice jumped. Eddie slipped off Alice's lap and started to bark like a mad thing, and the lady sitting behind them on the stairs began to giggle.

"You need a disguise."

"Miss Lane! You scared us!"

"Sorry, Maisie. You were talking so secretively — I just crept up and sat down on the next step." Miss Lottie Lane (otherwise known as the Darling of the Duke's Theater, or London's Favorite Lass, depending on where she was playing) fetched a paper bag of mint bonbons out of her skirt pocket and handed them around. "Anyway, why do you need to go spying at the butcher's? Have they been giving your gran short weight?"

"No, it's worse than that." Maisie explained about George. "He was always quite nice when we were at school. And I really liked Lucy, his sister. I'm worried about her, if he doesn't have a job anymore." She frowned.

"Oh dear . . . Yes, I see . . ." Miss Lane nodded.

The doorbell jangled below, and Alice leaped up. "Miss Sidebotham's back. See you next week, Maisie! I wish we bought our meat from Harrowby's—then I could watch and see when George gets his job back. You will solve it, I know you will." She hugged Maisie quickly and darted back into Madame Lorimer's rooms. Maisie could hear her speaking French quite loudly, to give Madame time to wake up.

"Come on, Maisie." Miss Lane took her hand. "Come up to my rooms. Oh, you can bring the dog—he's a sweetheart. Then you'll be staying out of the way of that awful governess—she doesn't approve of me in the slightest. She won't even say good afternoon if I pass her on the stairs. And I've got an idea." She whisked back up the stairs and Maisie and Eddie followed her.

Miss Lane's rooms smelled of expensive scent, faded flowers, and face powder. There were mirrors and framed photographs all over the walls, and clothes everywhere. Gran hardly ever sent Maisie up here to dust, as there was too much stuff on top of everything for dusting to do any good.

"Just put those on the floor, Maisie." Miss Lane waved vaguely at a pile of clothes on a chair, and Maisie frowned.

"I'd better hold them, Miss Lane. Eddie'll think they're for him to sleep on. He curls up on anything you put on the floor."

"Good point." Miss Lane snatched the pile and tucked it onto a shelf with some silver-framed photographs. "Right. Now sit. Like I was saying, Maisie, you need a disguise! You need to go undercover!"

"Dress up as someone else?" Maisie asked

slowly. She'd never thought of that. She wondered if Gilbert Carrington ever went about in disguise. "That's a brilliant idea . . ." she murmured. "If I were dressed as a boy, perhaps, I could go and ask at Harrowby's if there were any jobs going! I might even be able to get a job—I can't see them keeping that Reg very long. That would be the best way to find out who was stealing the money, wouldn't it?"

Miss Lane giggled. "Your gran might have something to say about that, though, Maisie. Aren't you meant to help out here?"

Maisie sighed. "You're right, I'd forgotten that. I don't think I could do two jobs and detecting as well. But it's still a good idea."

"I don't think you're being adventurous enough," Miss Lane said firmly, pulling out a wooden box full of strange waxy pencils wrapped in gold foil. "I can make you look like anyone you want, with greasepaint. It's better viewed from a distance, of course, when you're on the stage, but still." She looked at Maisie with her head on one side. "I'll show you. You'll not recognize yourself. Sit still."

She flung a sort of canvas cape around Maisie's shoulders and bundled her curly red hair back with a ribbon. For the next ten minutes, every time Maisie tried to say anything, Miss Lane would shriek at her to keep still. At last, she wound something soft and feathery around Maisie's neck and stood back like an artist examining her work. She chuckled to herself and looked around for a hand mirror.

Eddie, who had been sniffing around under all the furniture and found the end of a box of crystalized fruits, sneaked guiltily back to see what they were doing. He stopped short in front of Maisie's chair and let out a horrified howl.

"No taste," said Miss Lane disgustedly. "You look wonderful, darling."

"It's all right, Eddie, it's still me. What do I look like?" Maisie asked Miss Lane anxiously. "Am I horrible?"

"Of course not!" Miss Lane finally found the mirror underneath a pile of newspapers, and handed it to Maisie.

"Oh!"

Maisie stared at the person in the mirror. She looked about twenty. And she didn't have red hair anymore. It was black, and swept up on top of her head! She was wearing a pink feather boa, and she had matching pink cheeks, and smart pink lips.

"I thought about blond," Miss Lane explained, "but not with your eyebrows, Maisie."

"I don't think I could go and ask questions at the butcher's like this . . ." Maisie murmured.

"Perhaps not," Miss Lane admitted. "Although it would be fun to try. It was just to show you, Maisie. I can teach you how to do it yourself, you know. Come and find me tomorrow and I'll make you look like a boy. I've even got the outfit, somewhere, I think, from a comedy turn where I had to be a newspaper boy."

"But aren't you busy?" Maisie asked. "I don't want to be in your way." She had been very well trained about not bothering the lodgers.

Miss Lane shook her head. "Not in the

mornings. Don't come and wake me too early, though." She took off the wig and the boa, and scrubbed at Maisie's face with a cloth and some cream. "There. Back to yourself again."

Eddie, who had been sitting at Maisie's feet staring up at her suspiciously, let out a little whine of relief.

Maisie laughed. "Yes, it's me." She jumped up and kissed Miss Lane on the cheek. "Thank you! I'll see you tomorrow!"

Chapter Six

"If we tuck your hair up into this cap, it might work . . ." Miss Lane eyed Maisie thoughtfully. "That's what I did for the show. We can pull some of your curls out round the sides, and it should look like a scruffy sort of boy."

"Scruffy is right," Maisie agreed. "All the delivery boys have hair like someone's attacked them with a pair of blunt scissors."

"And just a bit of greasepaint. To make you look more tanned. Or dirty—it could be either." Miss Lane rubbed at Maisie's face artistically. Then she frowned. "Are you sure you're going to be all right, Maisie? You will be careful?"

"Course I will," said Maisie firmly. She was feeling a little bit nervous—her stomach seemed to be turning over inside her—but at the same time she was excited. Being out in disguise seemed like being a real detective. And she was sure that hanging around Harrowby's as a boy would be much easier than it had been as herself.

"Don't forget to lower your voice," Miss Lane reminded her. "You're a bit squeaky for a boy."

"Thanks, miss," Maisie said gruffly.

Miss Lane snorted with laughter. "Oh,

Maisie! That sounded like an ancient gravedigger with a cough! Somewhere in between."

Maisie sighed. "Yes, miss," she agreed, roughening her voice just a little bit.

"Much better." Miss Lane twitched at the greasy cap. "Now be careful that your gran doesn't catch you and think you're a burglar."

Maisie crept down the stairs, listening carefully for Gran and Sarah-Ann. She was pretty sure they were both in the kitchen, so she was going to make for the front door. She rolled her eyes. Most detectives would be trying to avoid master criminals, not their own grandmother. She paused on the first-floor landing, peering down over the banisters, with Eddie looking around her ankles. She was still wearing her own boots, but she needed to remember to smear some mud on them once she got outside.

"Are you bringing a message, young man?"

Maisie whirled around in horror . . . to see Professor Tobin standing in his doorway. "Oh!"

The professor peered at her. "Miss Maisie?"

"You recognized me . . ." Maisie said sadly. Her disguise hadn't worked at all.

"No, no. I recognized the dog," Professor Tobin assured her.

"Thank you for helping me keep him," Maisie said shyly. She had slipped a note under Professor Tobin's door to say thank you for the amazing wombat trick, but she hadn't seen him since.

The professor chuckled. "You were lucky I had something the right sort of size. Maisie, why are you dressed as a boy?"

Maisie sighed. She didn't think he'd tell on her. "I'm going detecting," she explained. "At the butcher's. They sacked George, the delivery boy, and I feel guilty because Eddie stole his sausages. They say George was stealing, but I'm sure it was someone else. I thought if I hung around the shop dressed as a boy, it would be easier to pick up any clues."

"Ah!" Professor Tobin nodded thoughtfully. "One moment." He nipped back into his rooms and returned with something in his hand, which he held out to Maisie.

"A magnifying glass!" she squeaked with delight. Her first piece of proper detecting kit—the notebook hardly counted. "Gilbert Carrington has one of these!"

"And all detectives should. You can keep it, Maisie. It's an old one, a little scratched, but still in good working order."

Maisie nodded gratefully. "Thank you, Professor. I'll take the best care of it."

"And just a hint, my dear," he said. "If you

want to be taken for an errand boy, your
nails are far too clean."

"Thanks, Professor Tobin," said Maisie.
"I'll dirty my nails at the same time as
I get my boots muddy." She tucked the
magnifying glass in the inside pocket of her
jacket—boys' clothes had so many useful
pockets!—and hurried off down the stairs.

"What do you want?" The boy loomed over
Maisie, who hunched up her shoulders
inside her too-big jacket.

"Just came to see about a job," she
muttered, trying to keep her voice low.

"What job?" Reg growled, and Maisie
backed away a little, glancing behind
her at the door that led out of the yard.
She'd sneaked in through the back of the

butcher's shop, thinking that a boy after a job wouldn't go in the front. But now it was only her and the horrible Reg here, and she wished she'd been more careful. Still, he really did think that she was a boy!

The only person Maisie had managed to see before Reg came into the yard with the bike was Sally, the girl who filled in the ledgers. She'd been leaning against the back door of the shop when Maisie first peered around into the yard. The older girl had a handkerchief up to her eyes, and she was sniffing, as though she'd been crying. Then someone had called her from inside and she'd dried her eyes and called that she was coming, in a very cheerful voice. Perhaps she'd had a fight with her young man, Maisie reckoned. Sarah-Ann had been just like that when the smart young policeman who patrolled Albion Street had been seen making eyes at someone else. They'd made up, eventually, but Sarah-Ann had cried into the washing-up for days.

Once Sally had gone, Maisie went right into the yard, hoping to get a chance to talk to her if she came out again, or one of the other assistants. She hadn't reckoned on Reg appearing.

"Heard there might be a job going," she said. "Heard someone got the sack."

"Yeah, he did, and I got his job, so you can just clear off." Reg put out one meaty hand and shoved Maisie at the door. She banged into the wooden frame, and clutched her shoulder.

Eddie barked furiously and jumped up, snapping at him. Reg tried to kick the little

dog away, cursing, and Maisie screamed,
"Eddie, no! Here!"

She was so scared that Reg might really
hurt Eddie that she forgot about lowering her
voice, and Reg glanced over at her, frowning.

"Hey . . ." he muttered, aiming one last
kick at Eddie, and then stomping toward
Maisie. "Who are you? I've seen that dog
before . . ."

Maisie grabbed Eddie, sucking in her

breath at how much her shoulder hurt, and ran for it.

She didn't stop running until she was in a quiet little courtyard several streets away, and completely lost. Maisie sighed and sat down on a bit of broken wall, rubbing her bruised shoulder. "That didn't go very well, did it?" she said to Eddie, stroking her cheek across the wiry dome of his head. "I probably shouldn't have brought you with me. Not after the professor recognized you as well. It was stupid." She hugged him tighter. "But I wouldn't have wanted to go all on my own," she admitted. "You're my faithful assistant."

Her faithful assistant licked her nose and jumped down from her lap, trotting along the side of the street and looking back for her to follow him.

"Oh! Do you know where we are?" Maisie got up. "I'm sure I've never been here . . ." She followed Eddie, watching as he sniffed here and there and padded along. Was this where he had lived, before someone had tried to drown him? Maisie shivered. He certainly seemed to know where he was going.

At last they came to a street that Maisie was almost sure she recognized. It was much busier than the lanes Eddie had been leading her through till now. He looked up at her happily, his tail wagging just a little, as though he hoped she was pleased with him.

"Oh! You're a very good dog," Maisie said lovingly. "Clever, clever boy."

Eddie's tail speeded up so much that it almost looked blurred, and then it dropped suddenly and tucked between his legs and he skittered back against the wall.

"What is it?" Maisie crouched down beside him, her heart thumping fast again. Her boys' clothes felt clammy and cold.

Slouching toward them was a tall, stoop-shouldered man with long, greasy gray hair. He had a battered bowler hat tipped down over his eyes, and his overcoat was torn and dirty. Beside him scurried a dog that looked remarkably like Eddie, except bigger. Even down to that strange, lopsided ear.

Eddie whined and he stretched out his head, staring hopefully at the other dog. Even their brown patches seemed to be in the same places.

The bigger dog pricked up her ears as she came closer, and let out a sharp little bark.

"Quiet, you!" snapped the man, but the dog just kept staring at Eddie.

"That's your mother," Maisie whispered. "It is, isn't it? She's so like you. And that must be the man who threw you in the canal."

She stood up, too furious to be frightened anymore. Too furious to think, as well. She jumped out in front of the man, and he pulled up short.

"Watch it, you stupid little brat! Get out of the way!"

"Did your dog have a puppy?" Maisie demanded. "Did you drown him?"

"What?" The old man stared at her. "Get lost."

"I won't!" Maisie snapped. "You tried to drown him! My Eddie! I rescued him out of a sack by the canal. You did, didn't you? Look at them!"

Until now, the bigger dog had been pressed tight against the man's side, her head hanging low, and her tail neatly tucked away. But now that Eddie was dancing and yapping in front of her, the older dog's tail was swinging from side to side. She was too worn out and sad-looking to wag it properly, but it was as close as she could get. She and Eddie were sniffing at each other, and Eddie's tail was wagging so fast, it was hitting against his mother's legs.

"What're you saying?" the man snapped. "Not against the law to drown a puppy. What's your game, nosy?"

"You're cruel!" Maisie shouted, remembering just in time that she was meant to be a boy and not to let her voice go high.

People were starting to watch them now, their heads turning as they passed by, and the old man snarled. He didn't want anyone noticing him, Maisie thought. "Shut up," he snapped. And almost before Maisie saw what he was going to do, he swiped at her, aiming to cuff her around the head.

She dodged, jumping away into the road, and the old man growled something and hurried off.

His dog lingered, licking Eddie's ears, until the man turned back, farther up the road, and yelled at her. "Get here, now!"

Maisie hoped the poor dog wouldn't go. She wasn't quite sure what she would do about another dog—Gran would go into convulsions if Maisie brought her home—but she'd manage somehow.

"Stay with us . . ." she whispered hopefully. "We'll run . . . He wouldn't catch us."

But the dog nuzzled Eddie one last time and then scuttled away, following the horrible old man around the corner of the street.

Maisie let out a shaky sigh, realizing she'd been holding her breath all this time.

Eddie stood in the gutter and whimpered, and Maisie rubbed his ears, then picked him up and cuddled him. "I solved my first mystery," she whispered. "Or you solved it yourself, Eddie. But it's the saddest mystery ever. I'm not sure I'll even tell Alice—it would make her cry." She rubbed her cheek against his wiry little head. "I'm glad he tried to drown you, though, so I found you and you didn't have to live with him. I wish I could have stolen your mum, too, but she was his dog. She wanted to follow him even though he was awful. Eddie, we should go home."

Eddie looked around at her as he heard the word, and then wriggled out of her arms and shook his odd ears firmly. Then he set off determinedly down the street and Maisie went after him.

Chapter Seven

The next morning, Maisie sat on the stairs,
which she was supposed to be sweeping,
and looked at the list in her notebook. Only
one name crossed off. It wasn't very good.
She needed to go out detecting again, but
this time in a different disguise. Being a boy
had proved to be just a little too dangerous.
She slipped the notebook back into the
pocket of her apron and lovingly patted

her magnifying glass. She still hadn't used it properly. Oh, she'd examined footprints in the yard, and she'd worked out that Madame Lorimer had eaten a cream puff and an Eccles cake from Norton's Fine Bakery, just by careful examination of the washing-up. But it wasn't the same as using the magnifying glass for an actual case.

She wished she could see the coins that the butcher had marked and laid as a trap in the cash box. Then the magnifying glass would really come in useful. She had read an article in Gran's paper about the new science of fingerprints. Amazingly, it seemed that every person in the world had prints that were different. Gilbert Carrington had spoken to the newspaper and said that prints were extremely useful to a detective. Maisie had tried to compare her own prints and

Sarah-Ann's, made on a water glass, but they were very difficult to see. She needed more practice, of course, but it would be easier now that she had the magnifying glass. There might well have been prints on those coins, if only she could have examined them.

There was no use in brooding over it now, though. Gilbert Carrington did most of his detecting just by looking at people, and Maisie knew she was good at that too. She would have to solve the case with her own eyes, not by any newfangled inventions. Hopefully, she could slip out later on . . .

Later that day, Maisie peered into the little mirror that Miss Lane had lent her, and then back down at the drawing. It was very clever—it was all about shadows, and using them to make one's face look completely different. Miss Lane had given her a few of the little sticks to use as well, and she had made Maisie promise to come back and tell her exactly what happened. She had an audition to go to or she would have insisted on doing the makeup herself.

Maisie had borrowed a dress and bonnet and shawl from Gran that morning, after she'd finished sweeping the stairs. They were old ones that Gran kept in a chest in the little attic room, so hopefully no one would notice they had gone. The bonnet had a sort of veil across the front, which would help with the disguise as well, and Miss Lane had told her that she must remember to walk as though her feet hurt.

Maisie had decided that it would be

easier to hobble realistically if her feet did actually hurt, so she'd put some stones from the yard into her boots. That way she couldn't forget.

She smeared a bit more of the yellowish color underneath her eyes, and decided it worked. She looked like herself still, but her face was hollowed and sunken, as though she'd lost some of her teeth. She looked familiar somehow. Maisie frowned at herself for a while, and then gave a gasp of laughter. She looked like Gran!

Then she peeped out into the passage and hurried past the kitchen, out through the yard to the street. She had left Eddie in her room with a new bone. Sarah-Ann was so grateful to him for scaring away all the enormous rats, which she was sure were just waiting to jump out at her, that she kept finding him little treats. Maisie had hidden the bone away until today — she couldn't possibly take Eddie with her, in case he was recognized again.

Sarah-Ann was upstairs cleaning, and Gran had gone out to Miss Mason's Household Agency to see about a new maid. The young policeman had been made a sergeant, and he'd come around to tell Sarah-Ann the day before. He'd asked her to marry him, and so she wanted to leave as soon as she could. She was going to go and keep house for the young policeman, and he wouldn't want her to work as a maid once she was married. Gran was very cross about it. She said she'd only just got Sarah-Ann trained up, and now she had to start again.

"Ow!" Maisie muttered, as soon as she was outside the yard. Her stone-filled boots really hurt. By the time she got to Harrowby's, she was going to have blisters. Still, it worked. She was tottering along like a little old lady.

"Are you all right, miss?" someone asked, and Maisie swung around guiltily.

"You looked a bit faint for a minute," the boy said, staring at her. "A bit wobbly."

Maisie peered through her dark veil, and stifled a laugh. It was George himself, looking down at her worriedly.

"I'm quite well, thank you," she said in a

quavery sort of voice. Then she straightened up and stared back at him. "George, it's me. Maisie. You know, from school. The one with the dog."

George squinted at her under the veil for a minute, looking bothered, and then frowned. "What are you dressed up like that for?"

"I'm investigating!" Maisie said, feeling slightly hurt. She was going to all this effort for him, and he was being grumpy about it. Then again, he didn't know that it was his case she was investigating. "I'm trying to prove it wasn't you that took the money. So you can get your job back. Unless you've got another job, of course."

George said nothing for a minute. Then he shrugged. "I haven't. No one wants a thief, do they? I do the odd errand here and there. But that's all. My mother's pawned all her good clothes to get money for food," he muttered miserably.

"There you are, then," Maisie said firmly. "We have to do something. I don't suppose you've got any idea who it was who took the money, now that you've had time to think about it?" she asked hopefully.

George shook his head. "Nope. Except . . . it had to be somebody who was there in the shop all the time. And that means one of the assistants. Alfred or Frank."

"Or Sally," Maisie reminded him. "Hmm, Alfred's Mr. Harrowby's nephew, though. I don't think he'd steal from the cash box when the shop's all going to be his one day. But we definitely need to watch Frank. What about Sally?"

"It could be her, I s'pose," George said. "But she wouldn't. She's Miss Perfect, she is. Got manners like a princess. She was always complaining that my nails were dirty. Or I was sniffing. I just had to stand there and she'd find something wrong with me."

Maisie could see her point, actually. George did sniff all the time, and his nails looked like he could grow potatoes under them. But she decided it wasn't tactful to say so. "Mmm. Well, I'll see anyway. Just because she's pernickety doesn't mean she couldn't be stealing."

"Thanks," George said gruffly. "Not that it'll work. But it's good of you to try."

Maisie wasn't actually planning to buy anything at Harrowby's. She didn't have any money, for a start. But she knew that Reg would almost certainly be out on his bicycle doing the deliveries, so she had come up with an idea so sneaky that it made her smile even to think of it.

She tottered into the butcher's shop, looking as frail and ancient as she possibly could, and practically collapsed over the counter.

"Oh dear . . ." Sally hurried around to her and caught her elbow. "Are you ill, madam?"

"I've had a shock . . ." Maisie quavered, glancing around and noting that one of the assistants—Frank, not Alfred—was leaning over the counter, looking at her worriedly. Good. Her two main suspects were there.

"Fetch her a chair," suggested one of the other customers. Frank brought Sally's stool while Sally went out to the pump to fetch a cup of water.

"Ohhhh," Maisie sighed loudly. "I'm bruised all over. That dratted boy!"

"Which boy?" Mr. Harrowby leaned over the counter to ask.

"On one of those newfangled bicycles," Maisie said, eyeing him under her veil. "Just over on Portland Avenue. He knocked me right over and didn't even stop!"

Mr. Harrowby frowned anxiously. "Er, a delivery boy?"

"Oh dear, yes, didn't I say?" Maisie explained feebly. "Your delivery boy. I saw the name, Harrowby's, painted on the dreadful machine. I thought I should tell you, you see . . ." She flopped back against the counter.

Mr. Harrowby groaned. "That Reg! I'll scrag him! I'll mince him up! This is the third time!"

Maisie blinked. This was even better than

she had expected! It also made her feel a bit less mean. George needed his job back, but that would be hard on Reg. But if he had actually been knocking other people down, not just nearly running her and Eddie over, then he deserved to go! And he'd really hurt her the day before, when he shoved her in the yard. She shook her head sadly. "I don't know why you got rid of the other one . . ." she said. "He was a dear boy. He helped me across the road once. And only last week I saw him chasing an awful dog that had stolen some sausages. A nasty, fierce brute! Your boy made such an effort to catch him."

"George did come back with a tale about a dog," Mr. Harrowby admitted. "But that was the day I let him go." He looked uncomfortably at Maisie. "Not because of the sausages. He'd been stealing . . ."

Maisie shook her head. "Surely not. Such a good boy."

"I think she's right," Sally put in. "I don't think it was George. He said he found that coin in the yard, and I think he was telling the truth. I don't see how he could have got at the money—he hardly ever came in the front of the shop."

She was twisting her fingers together anxiously, Maisie noticed, and looking down at the floor, as though she didn't want to catch anyone's eye. How odd that she should stick up for George when she had always complained about him, Maisie thought.

She looked carefully at Sally, trying to think like a detective. It really had to be her or Frank. So could Sally be involved? But why? Surely it would be stupid for her to steal from Harrowby's? She was bound to be suspected when she was the one who handled most of the money. She would have had to be desperate.

Sally's boots were pretty, Maisie thought. A dark leather, with a pattern of little holes stamped around the toes. They must have been quite expensive, but now the leather was cracking, and the heels were worn down—as though she didn't have the money to get them mended.

Maisie felt her breath catch

in her chest. It was a clue! A real clue! She just wasn't quite sure what it meant. She needed to go home first and think it all through. Maisie blundered up from the stool. "Thank you for the water, dear . . ." she murmured. "I'll be off now."

"Are you sure?" Mr. Harrowby muttered anxiously. He was obviously worried she was going to keel over on the way.

"Quite sure." Maisie limped out of the shop, trying hard to look old and feeble. She felt quite feeble, actually. This disguise thing was very hard work.

Chapter Eight

"I don't think it can be Alfred," Maisie
muttered to herself as she swept the hallway
floor. "But Sally does seem suspicious. It
does look like she's short of money . . ."
She whipped her notebook out of her apron
pocket to look at her list of suspects. "What
about Frank, though? I didn't even have a
chance to talk to him."

Eddie peered at her between the

banisters, his
eyes wide and
solemn.

"How am
I supposed to
find out if he's
honest?" Maisie
asked the dog.
"I can hardly
ask him. And I'd
rather not go to Harrowby's again, even in
disguise. People are going to get suspicious."
She frowned, leaning on the broom. "I need
a test . . . Like old Mr. Harrowby's coin
test, but one that actually works . . ." She
smiled thoughtfully to herself, and suddenly
started sweeping much faster. If she could
get this floor done, Gran might not mind if
she popped out. It was about the time that

Harrowby's would be shutting up shop and Frank would be on his way home . . .

Twenty minutes later, Maisie was hurrying up Albion Street toward the shops, with Eddie at her heels and a big wicker basket over her arm. As she reached Harrowby's, she strolled past, glancing sideways to try to see in without being too obvious. Ah! Alfred, Mr. Harrowby's nephew, was just putting out the gaslights, and Frank was winding a muffler around his neck, ready to set out into the chilly evening. Maisie darted around to the little alleyway and lurked there with Eddie. She was pretty sure that Alfred and Frank had already locked the front door of the shop and they'd be going out the back, through the alley. She just had to make certain that she was a little way in front of Frank as he set off down the road.

Maisie could hear the two young men talking as they came out of the back of the shop. They were discussing the stolen money, and her ears pricked up.

"Uncle's determined to get to the bottom of it. He was convinced it was that dratted boy George, but Sal and that old lady set him doubting again."

Maisie grinned to herself.

"He's right! What if whoever it was starts again? And I don't like the way we're all so suspicious of each other. If it wasn't that boy George, your uncle's right to want to find the real culprit."

Maisie nodded thoughtfully. That was Frank talking. He certainly didn't sound like a thief, lying low. He wanted the mystery solved too. She slipped her hand into her pocket and patted her magnifying glass. She might not have used it to look for real clues yet, but just having it made her feel like a proper detective. It gave her confidence.

As Frank and Alfred came out of the yard and headed up the alley toward Maisie, she slid out of the shadows and back onto the main street. She had to guess which way Frank would be going home. If she got it wrong, she'd have to double back and try to get in front of him again, which would be difficult. She hovered hopefully in the doorway of the draper's shop, which already had its shutters down, watching the yellowish light from the gas lamp in front of the butcher's. The two young men nodded to each other as they came out of the alley.

"See you tomorrow then, Frank!" Alfred called, heading away down the street. Maisie gave a triumphant little hop and hurried out

of the doorway in front of Frank, balancing
the heavy basket she'd brought.

She could hear him trudging along a
little way behind her, whistling to himself.
Just as she reached the next gas lamp,
Maisie pretended to trip over Eddie's string

lead, and tipped out the contents of her basket. Her one solitary shilling, her wages from Professor Tobin, went bowling down the flagstones toward Frank, while Maisie muttered crossly to herself and picked up the bits and pieces she'd borrowed from the kitchen — a tin of sardines, some laundry, and a few new-looking cloths.

If Frank did turn out to be less than honest, then this was going to be an expensive bit of detecting. Leaving the shilling waiting for Frank to spot in the lamplight, Maisie pattered on down the street.

"Miss! Miss!"

"Me?" Maisie turned and stared back at him hopefully.

"You dropped this!" He came hurrying up to her, smiling and wiping her shilling

on the hem of his shabby jacket before he
handed it to her.

"Oh! Thank you! My gran would have
been ever so cross if I'd lost her money."
Maisie bobbed him a little curtsey and
darted off, smiling to herself at the success
of her investigations.

So Frank wasn't a thief. He could easily have pocketed that money, and the poor girl who'd "dropped" it would never have known. So, if *he* hadn't taken the money, and Alfred wouldn't have wanted to, and George was innocent . . . there was only one person left.

The sweet, nice-mannered, ladylike Sally. But why? And how on earth was Maisie going to prove it?

"Er, is Maisie there, please?"

"Who wants to know?" Sarah-Ann giggled at the boy on the doorstep. It was late the next day. "Maisie! You've got an admirer at the door!" she called.

"Am not," George muttered.

"You've got the bicycle!" Maisie shrieked

as she saw it in the yard. "They gave you the job back!" She almost hugged him, but decided he would die of embarrassment. Eddie twirled happily around their feet, and George even patted him.

"Don't know what you said to Mr. Harrowby yesterday, but it worked. He came around to ours last night and offered me the job back. Thanks, Maisie."

"So, who did take the money, then?" Maisie asked thoughtfully. "Has he found that out?"

George shrugged. "Nope. No one knows." He eyed her anxiously. "Don't go snooping around, Maisie. I'll lose my job again if Mr. Harrowby works out you aren't really an old lady."

Maisie frowned. "But don't you want to find out? What if they do it again?"

George shuffled his feet and sighed. "Suppose so. Just be careful, though, Maisie, please?"

"You can help," Maisie pointed out. "You're on the spot. You can gather the evidence."

George didn't look very excited about this idea. "I can't go asking questions, Maisie. I already got Sally crying all over me, because I told her there was a rip in her skirt. Thought she'd like to know, that was all! I'm keeping my mouth shut—it's safer."

"Her skirt's torn . . ." Maisie muttered. "And her boots are all worn out. She needs money, doesn't she? But why? If she's the one who took the money, wouldn't she have used it to get her nice boots mended?"

"You don't suspect Sally, do you?" George asked.

"I don't know," Maisie sighed. "It's all such a mystery. I know you said she's very proper and fussy, but there really isn't anyone else. I dropped a shilling in front of Frank and he gave it back to me. He even polished it first! If he won't even take money that someone's dropped, I can't see him stealing from the shop."

"I suppose so," George said. "Maybe Sally could have spent the money on something else," he added, shrugging.

"I know that!" Maisie rolled her eyes. "What, though? That's what we have to find out."

"Well, you can ask her," George said firmly. "I'm not. She's scary. She takes after her mother."

"Her mother? What do you mean?" Maisie looked at him in surprise.

"Sally's mother. She's a right old witch. She used to come to the shop sometimes to fetch Sally. She works at the grocer's down the road, or she used to, anyway. Sally's little sister's ill, I think, and she has to stay at home to look after her. Haven't seen her in a while."

Maisie stared at him. "But that's it!"

George looked blank. "What is?"

"It's expensive to be ill." Maisie shuddered, remembering last winter when Gran had a cough that wouldn't get better. That was when Gran had first kept her home from school to help in the house, because she couldn't manage with just herself and Sarah-Ann. "Doctors cost a lot. Ever such a lot."

"You mean she could have stolen the money to pay for a doctor?" George muttered, frowning. "You might be right. Makes sense. She's got to keep them all now, hasn't she? Now her mum's not earning."

"I bet if we could find out which doctor it was and get into his house, or look in his pockets, we'd find the rest of those marked coins . . ." Maisie looked thoughtful, and George stared at her in horror.

"Maisie Hitchins! I've only just got my job back. I'm not going pickpocketing a doctor!"

"But one of us could pretend to be ill, and . . . Maybe not." Maisie stopped for a moment. "And we can't tell anyone, George. If Sally loses her job, what's going to happen to her mother, and her sister?" Maisie sighed. It was a great pity to solve a mystery so nicely and not be able to boast about it. "And we haven't any proof, anyway. It'll just have to stay a mystery."

George nodded. "Not sure how long that'll work, though. Mr. Harrowby, he's sniffing about . . . now that he doesn't think it was me after all."

"Maisie! Are you still gossiping with the butcher's boy?"

"That's Gran," Maisie said apologetically.

"I've got to go. Look, do me a favor, will you?"

George looked at her suspiciously. "What sort of favor?"

"Just ride back down Laurence Road, that's all. And when you get to the big house on the corner with Charwell Row, go slow and wave. A friend of mine lives there." Maisie smiled to herself. Hopefully Alice would be looking out the window.

Chapter Nine

"Can I go too, Gran?"

Maisie's grandmother paused in the middle of tying on her bonnet and turned around to stare at her. "Go shopping? You want to go shopping?"

Maisie nodded. She'd known Gran wouldn't believe her.

"Maisie Hitchins, if you're sweet on that butcher's boy, I shall send you to stay with your great-aunt in Devonshire."

"I'm not!" Maisie sighed. "Honestly!" But she could tell that her grandmother wasn't convinced. "There's something funny going on at Harrowby's. Someone stole some money. It's interesting . . ."

"In other words, you're nosing," Gran snapped. "Still, anything to teach you how to shop properly, Maisie. Get your hat." She glared at Eddie, who was sitting by the stairs looking hopeful. "I suppose that creature can come with us."

"Oh, thank you, Gran! He's got a proper lead now—I bought him one with the money Professor Tobin gave me for cleaning out Jasper." She showed off the thin leather lead—she'd bought it at the saddler's. It had only cost fourpence, so she'd slipped the other two pennies into the best teapot, where Gran kept her housekeeping money. Luckily she hadn't complained about the extra sausages on the butcher's bill, and now they were paid for.

On the way to Harrowby's, Maisie tried to explain about the money, and how George had lost his job and got it back. It was quite hard to tell the story without mentioning being a boy, or borrowing Gran's old dress and bonnet!

"So you think it was this girl? Poor child."

"But she let George get sacked!" Maisie pointed out.

"Because she was trying to do her best for her sister, Maisie!" Gran sniffed. "Of course she shouldn't have done it, but still. Goodness, what's happening here!"

They could hear the shouting from halfway down the street. Several passersby were lingering outside the butcher's shop, peering in curiously.

Mr. Harrowby was standing in the middle of the shop, bellowing like a bull. His black mustache was shooting up at the ends as he yelled, and Sally was huddled back against the window, crying, while a couple of fascinated customers stared.

Maisie hurriedly tied Eddie's lead to the ring outside the butcher's and then darted in after Gran.

"A common thief!" the butcher roared.

"Oh, no! I'm so sorry . . . I never meant to—I wanted to give it back. I've saved my wages. I thought I could put it back before anyone really noticed. Elsie's getting ever so much better now . . ." Sally sobbed, holding out a battered little leather purse.

Maisie caught George's eye—he was standing at the door out to the back of the shop, watching. They nodded to each other. Elsie must be her little sister. They'd been right. But poor Sally . . .

"Mr. Harrowby!" Gran snapped. "What's the use of shouting at the poor creature?"

"Poor creature? She's a criminal. I won't have her working here." The butcher snatched the purse, and then folded his fat arms and glared. "Get her coat, Alfred!" he cried. "There. Out!"

Gran shook her head crossly, and flapped her skirts at Alfred when he dared to come close to Sally. "Her little sister's been ill!" she snapped. "The girl was only trying to protect her family."

"With *my* money!" the butcher growled.

"She was going to pay it back!" Maisie put in. "You've got your money now!"

But Mr. Harrowby turned on her, still roaring so loudly that Maisie felt as if she might blow over. "She should have asked for help! Not stolen my money in the first place!"

"I did try to . . ." Sally gasped. "You said I'd have to wait to buy a new dress next payday — you wouldn't listen when I tried to explain about Elsie."

"She has given it all back . . ." Alfred started to say. "Perhaps we should let bygones be bygones . . ."

But Mr. Harrowby went even redder and let out a furious snort. "Nonsense! No such thing! Get out of here, girl!"

"Ridiculous. The man clearly won't listen

to reason. Come along, girl." Gran took Sally's arm and marched her out of the shop and down the road a little. "Here, have a handkerchief."

"What am I going to do?" Sally wailed.

"You're going to come back home with us and have a nice cup of tea," Gran said firmly. "Stop that crying, it's not doing you any good at all."

She hurried them all back to Albion Street and through the backyard into the kitchen. "Get that kettle on the stove, Sarah-Ann!"

Sarah-Ann stared as Maisie and her gran pushed Sally into a chair. "Isn't that the girl from the butcher's?" she murmured to Maisie. "What's happened to her?"

"I've lost my job!" Sally whispered miserably. "And now I'll never find another one . . ." She buried her face in the handkerchief Maisie had passed her from the ironing pile.

"Can you cook? And wash dishes?" Gran eyed her thoughtfully as she fetched milk from the larder. "Sweep floors? It's not what you're used to, but needs must, dear."

Sally glanced up from the handkerchief and nodded tearfully. "I'll do anything. Elsie's better, but she still needs looking after. Ma can't work. I need to be earning."

"Someone to take Sarah-Ann's place!" Maisie gasped, seeing what Gran was thinking. "I never thought of that."

Her grandmother turned from the hot plate on the stove, and smiled. "No, Maisie. But you don't have *all* the brains in the family, dear. And don't think that this means I approve of you poking your nose into other people's business!"

Maisie smiled at her. Gran sounded sharp, but Maisie knew she didn't mean it. If she'd really been cross, she wouldn't have been making Maisie cocoa, which was a special treat. Gran handed her the steaming cup and poured out tea for herself, Sally, and Sarah-Ann.

Maisie sipped her chocolate, looking down as Eddie nudged against her feet. He'd gone to fetch his bone, and now he was watching Gran carefully, to see if she would send him out of the kitchen. But she was pretending she hadn't noticed him, so he slumped down on Maisie's boots, with one paw stretched lovingly around his precious bone.

Maisie smiled to herself and listened to Gran telling Sally the long list of jobs she would have to do as a maid. She and her faithful assistant had solved their first two cases. They didn't sound quite as dramatic as Gilbert Carrington's adventures, of course. They'd hardly get written up in the newspapers, like the Larradine Rubies. But Maisie was sure that they were every bit as important. And that Gilbert Carrington would have been impressed with her detecting.

She reached down to stroke Eddie's ears and sighed happily. She hoped that there would be another mystery to solve soon . . .

Coming in 2015

The Case of the Vanishing Emerald

Lila Massey, famed star of the stage, is distraught—her beau, a mysterious young man, gave her a priceless emerald necklace, and now it's missing! Maisie is instantly intrigued and decides to investigate the suspects at the theater. But nothing is what it seems in this world of make-believe . . .

To find out more about Holly Webb visit

www.holly-webb.com